WELCOME TO THE ISLAND

by Dela Costa   illustrated by Ana Sebastián

LITTLE SIMON

New York London Toronto Sydney New Delhi

LITTLE SIMON

An imprint of Simon & Schuster Children's Publishing Division

1230 Avenue of the Americas, New York, New York 10020

First Little Simon hardcover edition December 2022

Copyright © 2022 by Simon & Schuster, Inc.

All rights reserved, including the right of reproduction in whole or in part in any form.

LITTLE SIMON is a registered trademark of Simon & Schuster, Inc., and associated colophon is a trademark of Simon & Schuster, Inc. For information about special discounts for bulk purchases, please contact Simon & Schuster Special Sales at 1-866-506-1949 or business@simonandschuster.com.

The Simon & Schuster Speakers Bureau can bring authors to your live event. For more information or to book an event contact the Simon & Schuster Speakers Bureau at 1-866-248-3049 or visit our website at www.simonspeakers.com.

Series designed by Laura Roode.

Book designed by Laura Roode. The text of this book was set in Congenial.

Manufactured in the United States of America 1122 LAK

10 9 8 7 6 5 4 3 2 1

Cataloging-in-Publication Data is available for this title from the Library of Congress.

ISBN 978-1-6659-2654-6 (hc)

ISBN 978-1-6659-2653-9 (pbk)

ISBN 978-1-6659-2655-3 (ebook)

Contents

ISLA'S SECRET

◆◆◆◆◆◆◆◆◆◆◆◆◆

Scribble, scribble, scribble, loooong scribble, swoop de loop.

Isla Verde bit the end of her pencil as she looked at her notebook. The sunlight in her backyard was just right.

Everything fit together perfectly on the island of Sol. Even the breeze blew gently, as if it were waving hello instead of scattering her pages.

"What do you think, Fitz?" Isla asked her best friend, Fitz the Gecko.

Oh yes, Fitz was a gecko. But he had also been Isla's bestie for as long as she could remember.

Fitz lay on a warm rock and took a long look at Isla's art.

"My tail isn't that long, you know!" he said.

Isla huffed. "It's called creative freedom! Plus, I'm not even done yet."

"Mmhmm. If you say so!" Fitz said.

He returned to his sunbathing, enjoying the heat.

Fitz and Isla's friendship was special, and not just because they did everything together. It was because they could *speak* to each other. In fact, Isla could speak to all the animals on Sol. This was Isla's secret. No one else knew.

Well, except all the other animals on the island . . . and now you. To Isla, communicating with all creatures was as natural as breathing.

"Okay, I have good news and bad news, Fitz," Isla announced. "Good news, I can redraw your tail."

"And the bad news?" asked Fitz sleepily.

"I've drawn you so many times today, I think I'm starting to see two of you," Isla admitted.

Fitz stood as if he was going to walk a runway show. "That sounds like good news all around. Who wouldn't want two of me?"

Isla let out a giggle. "Fitz, hold that pose! It's perfect!"

The gecko groaned. "Isla, you *know* I need my beauty sleep. Why don't you visit the tree frogs? I hear they're planning a croaking concert tonight."

Isla nodded. "Trust me, I know. I wanted to be their DJ, but tree frogs don't like to share the stage."

"They *are* experts in their craft," Fitz replied.

Isla listened for the tree frogs, but she heard a new noise instead.

Beep! Beep! Beep!

"What is *that*?" Fitz asked as he jumped up from his rock.

"That, my friend, is a truck," Isla said.

And it wasn't just any truck . . . it was a *moving* truck.

"New neighbors!" Isla cried out.

There were only three houses on Isla's street: Abuelo and Abuela's home, Mama and Isla's home, and then a third lonely house where no one lived. The house was rough around the edges, but nothing a new family couldn't fix up.

And it looked like they had arrived.

"Fiiiiiiiiiitz," Isla sang, clapping her hands. "You know what this means."

"Oh, no," Fitz said. "You want me to march on over there and be your tiny spy. I'll go—but if I get a whiff of dog breath, I'm out!"

Isla grinned widely. "Aw, you're the best!"

"Yeah, yeah," Fitz grumbled as he slipped away onto a tree and toward the new family. A few leaves fell behind him, landing in Isla's hair.

Fitz liked to pretend everything was too much work, but Isla knew he loved new adventures just as much as she did. And this was the start of the biggest adventure of Isla's life.

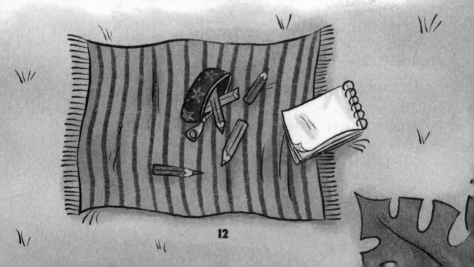

HUMAN FRIENDS

◊◊◊◊◊◊◊◊◊◊◊◊◊

Mama stood by the kitchen window as she watered her plants. Stepping into the Verde home was like stepping into nature. It was fresh, welcoming, and full of beauty.

Isla rushed inside, grabbed a stool from the corner of the kitchen, and plunked it next to the window.

"Mama, I have news!" she announced.

Mama put down her watering can and smiled at Isla's grass-stained clothing.

"Looks like you've had a busy morning," she said. "Now, what's the big news?"

"Look outside—it's a moving truck!" Isla squealed with excitement.

"Wow, that *is* exciting!" Mama said as she joined her daughter. "We haven't had neighbors in ages."

Isla leaned closer to the window, nearly pressing her face to it. "And look! A family, just as I suspected."

Three people came out of the house: a mom, a dad, and a young girl.

Mama patted Isla on the back. "Looks like she could be your age, *mi cielo*! Maybe even your future best friend?"

Isla watched the new girl and crinkled her nose.

"Fitz is already my best friend," she said. Then she added, "And you, Mama! Definitely you. And come to think of it, there's an iguana named Mia who lives a few streets over who's pretty great, but I don't want her to get too clingy so I just admire her from afar."

Mama laughed. "I still think it would be nice to meet a *human* your age. You know, a friend you can talk to and they actually talk back."

I do *have friends who talk back*, Isla
thought. *It's just that only I can hear
them.*

The new girl definitely stood out
in the neighborhood. She was like a
walking commercial for the color pink:

pink skirt, pink shirt, pink sandals, and even the pinkest bubblegum Isla had ever seen. It was all very . . . tidy. Tidy meant never getting dirty. Tidy meant all your clothes were brand-new. And to Isla, tidy meant boring.

Isla wondered how the new girl could ever go on adventures without getting even a little bit dirty.

At that very moment, Isla felt the need to meet her new neighbor. She had to know who the girl was and what she was all about!

"Well . . . ," Isla said slowly as she picked up a small potted plant from the kitchen shelf. "Let's give them this rare beauty and say hello!"

"Ah, that's a great choice." Mama approved with a humming smile.

"Perfect," said Isla as she marched toward the door. "But Mama, maybe you should leave your gardening apron at home."

Isla thought first impressions should be a *little* tidy.

"Of course." Mama slipped off her apron and placed it on the counter. "And while we are at it, maybe you should leave the leaves in your hair at home?"

Isla tilted her head and gave it a shake. "If you insist."

Mama helped pluck out a few stubborn ones. "That's better. Now let's go make some new human friends!"

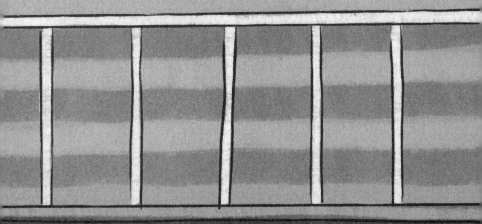

HELLO, NEW NEIGHBOR

◇◇◇◇◇◇◇◇◇◇◇◇◇

Isla led the way with the potted plant as they approached the porch where the girl's parents sat.

"Hi there!" Mama greeted them. "We're the Verde family, your new neighbors!"

Instantly, Isla noticed the girl in pink was missing. But her parents waved eagerly.

"This is for you," Isla said, handing over the plant.

"Oh," the mom said. "This is lovely. Thank you! Please, join us."

Mama sat down, and luckily Fitz appeared to save Isla from adult talk.

He jumped from the porch to her hand, wheezing. *"Phew!* This house . . . is . . . *huge.* I mean, everything is huge to me but those stairs were a workout!"

Isla stepped away from the porch and whispered from the side of her mouth, "Did you find anything interesting? A roller skating rink? A home aquarium? Built-in beehives?"

"These are all fun ideas," Fitz said, still out of breath. "But no. I'm happy to say that they don't have a dog. Oh, and I saw the most delicious bright yellow bananas in the kitchen."

"Focus, Fitz! What else did you find?" Isla snapped her fingers.

Fitz wiped the drool from the side of his mouth. "Sorry! I'm snacky. Okay, the girl's room is pink. It's like she invented the color."

"Makes sense, makes sense." Isla had guessed as much.

Just then, a scream made them stop and turn their heads.

"EW! A SLIMY FROG JUST CROAKED AT ME!"

A blur came running from the backyard and nearly slammed right into Isla!

It was the new girl. And she looked
very surprised to see Isla's face.

"Sorry," she said. "There was this
icky frog and . . . wait. Who are you?"

"Me?" Isla asked. Then she looked down at Fitz, and he nodded. "Of course me. I'm Isla Verde. Nice to meet you!"

"I'm Tora Rosa," the girl said. She held out her hand out for a shake, then quickly changed her mind. "Um . . . don't freak out or anything, but there's a *thing* sitting on your shoulder. If you stay still, I can scream for my dad to get it off."

Isla frowned. "Thing? What thing?"

"That weird lizard thingy. Don't you see it or *feel* it?" Tora pointed at Fitz.

"Our cover is blown!" Fitz leaned down and wiggled his tail. "Just say the word and I'll pounce!"

"Be nice," Isla whispered to Fitz.

"Excuse me?" Tora asked.

"Sorry, I was talking to Fitz," said Isla. "He's my best friend in the entire universe. And hey! You know your lizards! He's a yellow-headed gecko, to be exact."

Tora looked surprised. "So . . . you talk to it?"

"He's not an *it*! And . . . um, no, I was just comforting him," Isla said. "Did you have any animal friends where you grew up?"

Tora shrugged. "Not really. We didn't have any animals where I'm from, other than squirrels or pets."

Isla's jaw dropped. How could anyone live in a world without animals?

"So then, what did you do for fun?" she asked.

"Lots of stuff!" said Tora. "We had shopping malls, spas, bakeries, movie theaters. . . . You know, city stuff. I'm from La Ciudad, after all."

"Ah, the big city!" Isla said with a nod.

Tora arched her back proudly and pointed to a shiny pin on her jacket. It read LA CIUDAD. "Yep. I'm a big city girl through and through," she said. "My aunt even gave me this pin, so I'd never forget where I came from."

Isla had never stepped foot in LA CIUDAD, but her Mama was born there before moving to Sol. From the stories her Mama used to tell her, Sol was *nothing* like the city.

Sol was amazing like that. Sometimes Isla was convinced it breathed and shifted on its own, creating new little spots for her to explore.

Tora scrunched up her nose. "To be honest, getting dirty isn't exactly my idea of fun."

"She's a tough one," Fitz whispered.

"That's okay! There's something here for everyone." Isla paused. "If you want . . . maybe you could come to dinner. Maybe tomorrow?"

Tora looked at Fitz, then back at Isla. "Uh, sure. I'll ask my parents. I should get back to unpacking and you should, maybe, get that gecko back to his home or whatever. See you around."

As Tora ran off, Fitz said, "Back home? Where does she think I live?"

Isla stroked the gecko's head. "Relax, buddy. We've got a dinner to plan."

THERE SHOULD BE (PINK) FLOWERS

◆◆◆◆◆◆◆◆◆◆◆◆◆◆

The next day, Isla lay on her bed thinking of how to make the best dinner ever for Tora.

She had never felt this nervous before. What if Tora *didn't* like all the plants at her house? What if she thought it was strange that Fitz ate at the table with them? What if Tora just didn't like her?

A chomping sound stopped Isla's racing thoughts.

"Worried about Tora?" Fitz asked in between chewing banana slices. "Just give her a chance to know the real you."

Isla's stomach was doing somersaults. "I don't know, Fitz. We seem so different. Maybe *too* different to be friends."

"You and I are totally different and we're best friends," Fitz reminded Isla.

He was right. Most of the creatures Isla knew were not like her at all. Mostly because she was a human and they were animals like birds, fish, reptiles, amphibians, dogs, cats . . . and on and on.

She sat up and Fitz nearly toppled backward. "Listen up!" Isla said. "We'll make sure that Tora has the most amazing time ever. And do you know how we're gonna do that?"

"With bananas!" Fitz cried out, holding a slice above him.

"So close!" she said. "We're going to make great food and get beautiful flowers. Can you guess what color?"

"Pink!" Fitz replied.

Isla winked. "See? We really do make a good team. Now let's go find those flowers!"

Isla scooped up Fitz and they made their way outside, where Isla's bike and turtle-shaped helmet sat. As she strapped on her helmet, Isla hoped the market had all the right answers.

CHAPTER 5

THE MARKET

◇◇◇◇◇◇◇◇◇◇◇◇◇

Isla could find adventure anywhere she went—and the town market was no exception!

She rode her bike the short way over, with Fitz peeking from inside the top of her woven basket.

"Hello, Isla!" merchants greeted her as she rode by.

Isla cheerfully greeted them back.

"Hi, Mr. Antonio! Hello, Mrs. Camila! Love what you've done with your hair!"

The market was bursting with life. Fresh fruits, vegetables, and handmade knickknacks poked out of the bags of shoppers. Tables overflowed with families feasting on delicious foods. Musicians played their tambourines and maracas. Sometimes, there were singers and everybody got up to dance.

Isla flew by the colorful fruit stands, jewelry tables, the pastry hut, the ice cream shop, and the newest bookshop. It was the perfect day—the breeze even sang with delight!

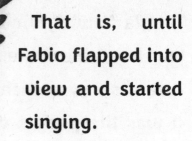

That is, until Fabio flapped into view and started singing.

Fabio was a laughing seagull who thought he had the most amazing voice.

"LAAAAAAAAAAA!" he belted loudly over stalls and tables.

People covered their ears and ran away to escape the awful sound, but that silly bird didn't get the hint.

"It hurts just listening to him," Fitz said, sliding a hand down his face.

"*Everyone* feels it, Fitz." Isla peddled faster to get away.

Finally, she reached the flower store in the corner and parked her bike.

Ding!

The bell rang as they walked through the door. She took in a deep breath and closed her eyes. The smell of all the greenery inside was wonderful.

The owner, Miss Flor, smiled warmly from behind the counter. "Great to see you again, Isla. Can I help you find anything today?"

"Yes, please," said Isla. "I need the biggest, best-smelling, most beautiful, most PINK flowers you've ever laid your eyes on!"

Before Miss Flor could reply, a voice behind Isla said, "I'd like to see those too!"

She turned to find Tora already in the shop. Suddenly the nervous feeling returned.

"It's you! Uh, Tora. Um, hi." Isla tripped over her words. "What brings you here?"

"Flowers," Tora responded, pointing at the shop sign.

Isla placed a hand on the counter, but it slipped off. "What! Us too!"

"Right . . . well, it *is* a flower shop," Tora said.

Isla froze. She couldn't think of *anything* else to say! It was like she forgot every word she'd ever learned *and* how to use her voice. Why was talking to other kids *so* hard? She'd never had this much trouble when talking to lake fish or jungle birds.

"Yikes! This is hard to watch," Fitz whispered as he covered his eyes with his tail.

Tora looked between Isla and Fitz. Then she broke the silence. "Why don't I wait outside while you pick out your gecko flowers or whatever?"

Isla groaned as the dinging door shut behind a zooming Tora. How had things gotten off to such a rocky start?

"Is it over? Can I look now?" Fitz asked, peeking over his tail.

It *was* over . . . unless Isla did something quickly.

FABIO

◊◊◊◊◊◊◊◊◊◊◊◊◊

Outside, Tora was standing beside a bike that was so pink, glittery, and bright that it made Isla squint. Even the tassels seemed to glow.

Isla's bike was on the ground next to it: green, a little rusty, and *very* muddy.

Tora was tracing the LA CIUDAD pin on her shirt. It glinted bright in the sunlight.

"Hey again," Isla said, waving shyly.

"Sorry about inside. I get nervous around new people, and you were the last person I thought I'd see in there. If you want to buy flowers, you can go first. Sometimes Miss Flor lets you help find all the ladybugs inside the flower shop."

A smile slowly blossomed across Tora's face. "I *do* like ladybugs."

"Really?!" Isla gasped.

"I've never actually touched one though, because *yuck*," Tora admitted. "You know what I mean?"

Isla *didn't* know what Tora meant, so she tried a different idea. "Then you could help with other things, like tying bows and making pretty bouquets."

LAAAAA!

Fabio's ugly squawking came closer and closer.

Tora covered her ears and cried out, "Whoa! What is wrong with that bird?"

Isla snorted. "How much time do you have? Basically, he thinks he's a pop star. It's very unfortunate."

"Oh my," Tora said with a grin. "Why is he in the market? I thought seagulls liked the beach."

"He follows the crowd," said Isla. "Or as he calls them, his adoring fans."

Tora laughed at Isla's joke and suddenly the day was getting better!

Until Fabio showed up for his solo.

"Well, well, well!" the bird called as he circled in the sky. "If it isn't Isla and Frank!"

"Fitz! The name's Fitz!" Fitz shouted.

"Same thing!" Fabio said grandly. "Oh, and what do we have here? A gift? For *me*?"

What came next came fast, as adventures on the island can do.

Fabio saw the glint of Tora's pin, then swooped right in to snatch it!

"My—my pin!" Tora cried, pointing at Fabio as he flew away. "That thing took the only part of the city I had left!"

Isla could hear Fabio's new, awful song ringing through the market. *"It's mine! It's mine! So shiny and divine! Poor wingless creatures, you'll never catch me!"*

Quickly, Isla grabbed her helmet and picked up her bike. "I know where he lives. You don't have to come if you don't want to. I wouldn't want you to get your bike dirty."

"Don't worry about my bike," Tora said, in a sudden gust of bravery. "Let's get that bird!"

A LITTLE SUSPICIOUS . . .

◊◊◊◊◊◊◊◊◊◊◊◊◊◊

As they rode through the market, Isla pointed out some of her favorite spots.

"They have the best ice cream. And the library is over there. Right now, I'm reading about how to grow plants in the dark. I mean, how cool is that?"

"Um, shouldn't we be paying attention to where that bird went with my pin?" Tora said.

"Oops, sorry!" Isla chuckled nervously. "I talk a lot when I'm excited. Like, see the tortoise? He can live over one hundred and twenty years! He says he's only a hundred ten, but look at him. And hey, he's not supposed to be in the road."

"Tortoise in the road?!" Tora shouted, breaks squealing as she hurried to stop.

Isla stopped too, then sighed heavily. "How many times do I have to tell you?"

"What? Who? Me?" Tora looked startled.

"No, sorry, not you." Isla slipped off her bike and walked over to the tortoise. "All right, Mr. Tortoise. It's not safe enough for you to keep crossing this bike path. I'm sorry, pal, but you're just not fast enough."

The tortoise huffed and puffed, as he usually did when Isla came to the rescue. "Back in my day, I was the fastest shell out here! I zoomed through every corner of this island in a blink of an eye!"

"I believe you, but that was a long time ago," Isla whispered. Then she helped him back to safety with her hands. "I'll bring you some fresh lettuce leaves tomorrow."

"Thanks, Isla," Mr. Tortoise grumbled, blushing. "I'm off to get more steps in today."

Isla laughed, then ran back to her bike. "I wish I could have seen Mr. Tortoise back in the day!"

Tora didn't seem to be as interested in finding the pin. Instead, her eyes curiously darted between Isla, Fitz, and the grumbling Mr. Tortoise.

"Were you . . . talking to that turtle?" Tora asked, her eyes narrowing.

"Tortoise, actually," Isla said, laughing nervously. "And no, no, I was definitely not talking to him. Just . . .

giving some friendly advice. But what does that matter? We're on a rescue mission!"

"Nice save," Fitz whispered.

Tora's motivation returned and she nodded bravely. "Right!"

CHAPTER 8

FABIO . . . AGAIN

◊◊◊◊◊◊◊◊◊◊◊◊◊

Fabio lived in an old wiry tree.

The tree was older than Mr. Tortoise and had lots of mud at the base of the trunk. There were tons of things that had washed up crowded in the mud. Or Fabio *said* they had washed up.

There were beach toys, seashells, jewelry, car parts, bike parts, boat parts . . . lots of parts.

"Fabio thinks of himself as a singer," Isla said to Tora as they parked their bikes. "He also likes collecting things, though your pin is probably the only thing he has worth collecting."

Tora pointed toward Fabio. "There's that bad bird!"

Tora stormed toward the tree, but Isla stopped her.

"Wait," Isla said. "We don't want to scare him away. You stay here and let me try something. Trust me, it's not the first time I've dealt with this cuckoo."

"Oh, I thought he was a seagull," said Tora.

Isla smiled. "Yeah, you're right. Now just relax, hang back, and let me do my thing."

As Isla walked to the tree, Fitz scrambled next to her over all the junk.

"Blegh!" the gecko gagged. "What is all this stuff?"

"It's my treasure!" Fabio snapped back. Then he held up Tora's pin with his stinky bird feet. "And now I have something new to add to my collection!"

"Fabio, you know why we're here," Isla said, holding out her hand. "Give us what we want."

Fabio took a deep bow. "Ah! Of course! You want a front-row ticket to my show? Sorry, kid, you can't afford me."

Isla groaned. "No, Fabio, we don't want to hear you sing."

Fabio choked dramatically. "Bah! Everyone wants to hear me sing!"

Fitz climbed onto Isla's shoulder and shook his tiny hand in the air. "We're here for Tora's pin, bird brain!"

"Oh, *you* again, *Frank*." Fabio twisted his long neck away. "Don't you have a warm rock to sleep on somewhere? Because you're such a *yawn*."

Fitz was fit to scream, but the mention of the word *yawn* always made him yawn.

"See!" said the bird with a cackle.

Isla stood her ground. "Do the right thing, Fabio. You're giving our island a bad name! If you keep that pin, Tora will always think of Sol as a terrible place to live."

Fabio gasped. "Now you're just being ridiculous. The island of Sol is the most wonderful place to live. Look at it. Then me, then it, then me, then it, and now me."

"*We* know that," said Isla. "But Tora doesn't. And if you're mean to her now, she'll go back to her old home and tell all the birds on you!"

"She wouldn't," cawed Fabio.

"Yes, she would," Fitz sang.

Fabio opened his mouth and paused. It looked as if he was about to say something snooty, but instead he smiled a bit *too* nicely.

"You win this time, Isla!" the bird said.

Then Fabio flew down and dropped the pin into Tora's hand. Tora, who was suddenly standing much closer to Isla, looked very, very startled.

"Looks like you have some explaining to do, Isla dear!" Fabio squawked as he flew away. "Ha, ha! So long!"

"Where are you even going!" Fitz shouted. "You live *here*!"

Usually, Isla would've cheered their win. But now she was face to face with her new friend—who had seen and heard everything.

CHAPTER 9

SECRET'S OUT

◇◇◇◇◇◇◇◇◇◇◇◇◇

The air was still. Isla gulped. Was she ready to share her secret? She didn't even know where to begin.

"Well?" Tora crossed her arms. "Are you gonna tell me what's really going on?"

Isla looked at Tora. A million excuses ran through her head, but she knew Tora deserved the truth.

"Okay, don't freak out, but . . ." Isla paused. "I can talk to animals. And they talk back. I thought it was normal until I realized that other kids weren't doing it. And all those kids looked at me a little funny. So it kind of became . . . a secret."

Tora was silent, and Isla worried that she would give Isla the same look as the other kids had. The look that says, *Why are you so weird?*

But that didn't happen. Instead, Tora nodded. "So you speak to animals . . . like we're speaking to each other right now?"

"Yeah," Isla said. "I'll show you. Fitz, show Tora your favorite dance."

The gecko wiggled side to side and did a spin on his tail.

Tora's mouth dropped open.

"Wanna try?" Isla asked. "Fitz can understand you, too."

"Really?" Tora thought for a moment, then said, "High-five, Fitz!"

Fitz jumped up and gave Tora a mini-gecko high-five.

Isla and Fitz held their breaths, waiting for Tora to run away screaming. She'd just touched a gecko, after all.

But Tora jumped up and down, clapping her hands. "It's like a fairytale! All princesses can speak to animals!"

"So . . . you don't think I'm weird?" Isla asked softly.

"No way!" Tora cheered. "You're the luckiest girl in the world!"

Isla thought her heart was going to burst!

"Yeah, I guess it is pretty great!" Isla smiled widely. "And remember the tortoise earlier? I was talking to him."

"That was kind of obvious." Tora laughed. "Even for me."

Isla grinned. "Ready to get out of here? Let's get our flowers and go home to eat."

"Yay, food!" Fitz plopped down. "Now you're speaking my language!"

WELCOME TO THE ISLAND

◆◆◆◆◆◆◆◆◆◆◆◆◆◆

That evening, the two families gathered in the Verde home for a home-cooked meal of honey-roasted figs and vegetables, wild rice, and freshly squeezed passion fruit juice. The pink flowers sat in the middle of the table.

For dessert, they had Isla's favorite: soft vanilla custard with caramel drizzled on top.

Fitz gazed at the custard with heart eyes and Isla slipped him a spoonful.

After dinner, their parents chatted in the living room and the two new friends brought out the lawn chairs and waited for the backyard tree frog concert to begin.

"They've been practicing all week," Isla whispered to Tora as the frogs began to appear on a flowery bush. "Literally *every* single night of the week. I haven't gotten any sleep."

"Ahem." A tree frog was staring at her with narrowed eyes.

Tora laughed. "This is so amazing. Do you know all of the animals on the island?"

Isla thought about it. "A lot of them. I'll introduce you."

Tora flashed a smile. "I'd like that very much."

"Hey, wait, have you seen Fitz?" Isla asked. She knew he wouldn't want to miss the concert.

Tora froze and she looked at Fitz's sleeping figure on her lap. "I think I found him."

Isla clapped her hands over her mouth. "Aw! He must really trust you!"

"Really?" Tora melted, and even gave Fitz a pat on his head.

"Ladies and sleeping gecko!" announced one of the tree frogs. "Welcome to the Tree Frog Choir concert. Please hold your applause until the end of the show, and, as always, keep your phones on silent and no pictures . . . unless it's my good side."

The frogs began their night song—one that could be heard through the whole neighborhood.

Tora nudged Isla. "What are they singing?"

Isla listened for a moment. "It's a song called 'Welcome to the Island.' They must have written it just for you."

Isla never imagined she'd find a new human friend to share her secret and attend tree frog concerts with. But that was the beautiful thing about Sol. There was something new waiting around every corner.

DON'T MISS ISLA'S NEXT ADVENTURE!

HERE'S A SNEAK PEEK!

◆◆◆◆◆◆◆◆◆◆◆◆◆◆

"Hey, Isla," said Fitz. "If a piece of blueberry pancake accidentally falls off your plate, I'd be happy to take care of it for you."

Isla Verde laughed at her little gecko buddy. They had been best friends for as long as Isla had known she could speak to animals. Which was a very long time—basically all eight years of her life.

"You have your own papaya slices," Isla said.

"True. But there's always room for more," Fitz said.

Then Isla heard a cheerful whistle that she knew very well. It was her Abuelo!

"He's early!" Fitz said in a panic. "I thought I had time for a nap or two before we left."

"No time for napping," Isla replied. "The cabana is waiting!"

"*Cielo*, are you ready?" Mama asked between sips of freshly brewed coffee.

Coffee was one of the adult mysteries Isla couldn't solve. It tasted gross, but grown-ups loved it. Maybe she would change her mind when she was older.

"Ready as ever," Isla said as she got